Sapphire
Fairy Tales

GEM CLASSICS LIBRARY

Retold by Jane Carruth

RAND McNALLY & COMPANY
Chicago • New York • San Francisco

Contents

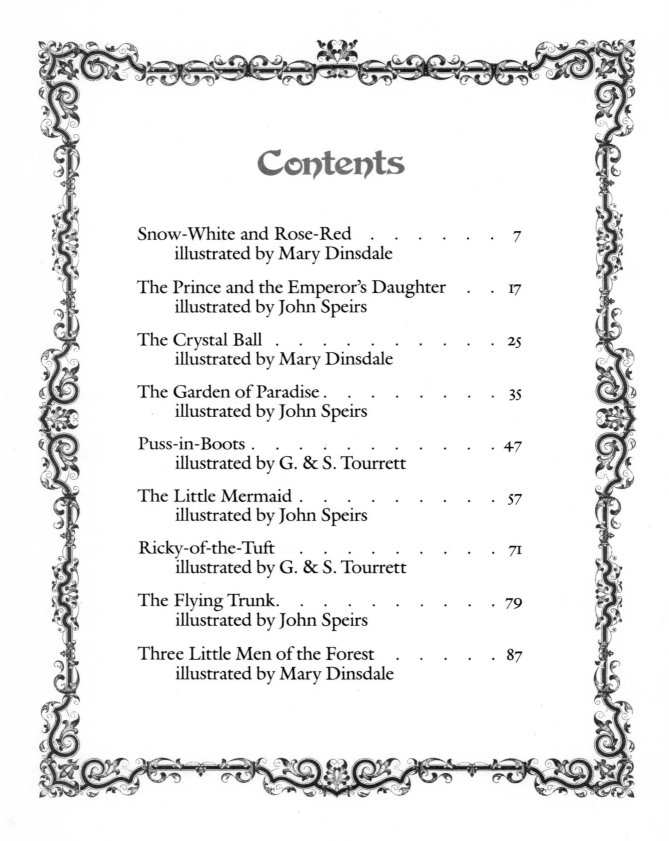

Snow-White and Rose-Red

ONCE UPON a time there was a poor widow who had a little cottage at the edge of a forest. Her greatest joy was two rose trees, one white and the other red, which grew in a small patch of garden. She named her two daughters after the rose trees, Snow-White and Rose-Red. Snow-White was quiet and gentle and helped a great deal in the house while Rose-Red was always gay and liked nothing better than to chase through the forest on sunny days.

But although the sisters were different, as sisters so often are, they were very close friends and were nearly always together. They had explored the forest so often that they were never afraid to go there on their own and sometimes the little rabbits would come and eat out of their hands.

In the summer, the girls would fill their basket with berries and talk to the shy little forest creatures. But in the winter, when the snow was on the ground, their mother would bolt the door and call them over to sit by the fire. Then, out would come her spectacles and Snow-White would give her the big book of stories and legends that they all loved. As they settled on a rug at their mother's feet, their pet deer would lie down beside them just as if he, too, wanted to hear a story.

One night, as they sat together around the fire, there was a loud knock at the door. "Go quickly, Rose-Red," said her mother, looking up from her book. "Some poor traveler must have lost his way in the snow."

When Rose-Red opened the door, there was a huge black bear, who thrust his head forward and said, "Will you let me come in? I won't do you any harm and I am nearly frozen to death."

Rose-Red screamed in fright and tried to shut the door, but her mother called out, "Let the poor bear come in, Rose-Red. You heard what he said. We cannot turn away any living thing on a night like this."

So Rose-Red opened the door wide and the bear stepped into the cottage. He stood on the mat, looking quite enormous in the tiny room. "Will one of you kindly brush the snow from my back?" he said. And, half-ashamed that she should have been so frightened, Rose-Red did as he asked.

Then Snow-White made a place for him beside the fire, and her mother said, "You may stay here as long as you want to. You are welcome to come as often as you wish during these hard cold months of winter."

There was no more reading from the book of stories that night for although the bear said very little, he allowed the girls to tug at his fur and pretend to roll him on his back. And, soon, even the timid deer was joining in the fun.

When it was time for bed, the widow said, "Stay here by the hearth where you will be nice and warm," and the bear nodded in a friendly way before stretching himself out on the rug.

In the morning, when Rose-Red ran into the kitchen, he was gone, but he returned early the next evening and once again they spent a happy time together.

All through the cold winter, the bear never missed a night and the girls grew to look forward to the evenings and to hearing his knock. But when spring came and the little birds welcomed Snow-White and Rose-Red into the forest with their songs, the bear said, "I must leave you now until winter comes again."

"Where will you go?" Snow-White asked sadly, scarcely able to hide her tears. "We shall miss you so much."

"Deep into the forest," the bear told her. "My treasure lies hidden there and I must guard it. In the winter the ground is hard and the wicked dwarfs who would steal it cannot dig it up. But in the spring and summer the earth is soft and the dwarfs dig deep burrows and steal all they can lay their hands on.''

How sad Snow-White and Rose-Red were to see the bear go and as they watched him trot away, Snow-White said, "It won't be the same now that he has gone.''

Some days later, their mother asked them to go into the forest and gather some wood. "You will enjoy the sunshine," she said, "and perhaps it will help you to forget the bear.''

As the two girls wandered along the paths, searching for sticks, they were suddenly surprised to see an odd little man whose long white beard was caught in the branches of a tree.

"Look!" whispered Rose-Red, "the tree must have fallen and trapped that funny little man by his beard.''

The little man, his face all lined and wrinkled like a crab-apple, was struggling desperately to free himself and when he caught sight of the girls, he screamed, "Fools! Idiots! Don't stand gaping! Help me, can't you?''

At this, the sisters bent down, took hold of the Dwarf's tunic and began to pull. But no matter how they tugged and pulled they could not free him. At last Snow-White took a pair of small scissors out of

her pocket. "It won't hurt," she said, and snip, snip, she cut off the end of his beard. "There!" she said, "now you are free."

If you are thinking that the Dwarf was grateful, you couldn't be more wrong. "Ruined! Ruined!" he screeched, hopping up and down holding his beard. "You've ruined my handsome white beard." And with a fierce scowl, he ran to a sack, which was filled with gold, threw it over his shoulder and stumped off into the bushes.

"Well!" said Rose-Red. "What a horrid little man! I wish we had left him alone."

"We had to help him," said Snow-White. "But I think he might have thanked us. Let's forget him and collect some wood."

But the girls were to see the Dwarf again much sooner than they expected. The very next day they went down to the stream to feed the wild ducks, and there he was again.

"It's the Dwarf!" Snow-White whispered, taking her sister's arm. "And he's in trouble again."

"So I see," said Rose-Red, although she didn't sound very sorry. "It looks as if he has been fishing and his beard has got tangled up in his line. Well, I don't care. This time I refuse to help."

But gentle Snow-White murmured, "I think we should try to get him free or else that huge fish at the end of his line is going to pull him right into the water."

"Then he'll get a soaking, that's all," said Rose-Red, rather heartlessly. The little man was in great danger of being pulled into the water, as she spoke, and he was now clinging desperately to some tall reeds. When he glanced up and saw the girls, he screamed, "Help! Help! Help me you – you idiots! Don't stand there like stupid sheep. Do something."

Snow-White and Rose-Red did as he said. They ran to him, and Snow-White took hold of his tunic and pulled. What a tug of war it was for the big fish was pulling too, to get free! But no matter how hard she tugged and pulled she could not free the little man. His beautiful white beard was so tangled up with the fishing-rod that nothing, it seemed, could move it.

"You know what you're going to have to do," said Rose-Red, as Snow-White, all out of breath, sank to the ground. "You're going to have to use your scissors again."

"I suppose I must," Snow-White said. And scrambling to her feet, she took out her scissors. Snip, snip, snip! Off came some more of the little man's beard.

The Dwarf was almost speechless with rage when he saw part of his precious beard lying on the grass. "You've spoiled my beard again!" he spluttered. "You did it on purpose!"

"We did not," cried Rose-Red. But the little man, his face all red and wrinkled with hate, glared at her so hard that she stopped, feeling suddenly frightened. Then, without another word, he went to a big stone and picked up a sack that lay behind it. As he heaved it up to his

shoulder, a handful of gleaming pearls fell out of it. Then he disappeared into the bushes.

Snow-White and Rose-Red said nothing of the unpleasant little Dwarf to their mother because they were afraid she might say they couldn't go into the forest.

"It isn't as if he could do us any real harm," said Rose-Red as they talked about him. "He is just horrid and ungrateful."

"I think he is wicked," said Snow-White, with a shiver. "And what is he doing with the gold and pearls? I don't believe they belong to him."

They were still talking about the Dwarf when their mother came into the kitchen the next day and asked them to go down to the village to buy some needles and thread.

Pleased at the chance of doing something for her and going out-doors, Snow-White and Rose-Red ran off through the forest, for that was the shortest way to the village. While they were still among the trees, they noticed a huge eagle soaring above their heads. Suddenly it swooped downwards and Rose-Red cried, "Oh dear, it must have seen something to eat. I hope it isn't after one of our little rabbit friends."

Then a familiar cry reached their ears: "Help! Help! Help me!"

"It's the Dwarf!" Snow-White cried, and she began to run. "The eagle must be after the little man."

The girls rushed into a clearing in the forest just as the big bird dropped down on the Dwarf and was preparing to carry him off. With a cry of horror, Rose-Red grabbed the little man's feet while her sister took hold of his beard. The eagle had no intention of giving up its prey too easily and the dwarf screamed in pain and terror as he was lifted off the ground. But the sisters hung on with all their strength until the bird gave up the struggle and flew away.

No sooner had the Dwarf recovered from his fright than he shook his fist angrily at Snow-White and Rose-Red. "Fools! Idiots!" he shouted at them. "You have torn my coat. My head aches with the way you pulled at my beard. Couldn't you take more care?" And he ran off, picking up a sack that lay half-hidden in the long grass.

"I don't care," said Snow-White. "I'm glad we saved him. Just imagine being carried off by an eagle!"

On their way back from the village, the sisters were surprised to come upon the little man again. Rose-Red pulled her sister behind a tree and they watched as he emptied one of his sacks on a flat stone. The precious stones shone like tiny stars in the bright sunlight and Snow-White let out a gasp of amazement.

The Dwarf whirled around immediately and saw them. "Spies! Robbers!" he shouted in sudden fury. "Be off with you!"

"We are not spies and we don't want anything from you," said Rose-Red, stepping out from behind the tree and facing the angry Dwarf. "So please don't shout at us."

"We have saved your life three times," said Snow-White, joining her sister. "And you haven't even thanked us."

Her words sent the little man into such a rage that he began hopping up and down, shaking his fist, and shouting at them to leave him alone. No wonder he failed to see the huge black bear come padding up behind him! When he did, it was too late to turn and run for the bear had grasped him in his broad paw. When he found himself a prisoner, the Dwarf's angry shouting changed to a pathetic whine.

"Spare me, Lord Bear," he whimpered. "I meant no harm. Take these precious stones – they are worth a fortune. And take those stupid girls there. They'll make you a much tastier meal than me."

Snow-White and Rose-Red clung to each other in terror for they

did not recognize the big black bear as their friend and playmate of the long winter evenings.

Still holding the Dwarf in his paw, the bear turned to them, saying, "I am your friend. Don't you know me?" As he spoke, he dropped his captive to the ground, killing him with a single blow from his great paw. Instantly, something strange and wonderful happened. In place of the bear stood a handsome young man, clothed in a suit of gold.

Snow-White and Rose-Red stared in amazement until the young man said, "The death of that wicked Dwarf has set me free from the spell he cast upon me. Out of greed he condemned me to wander through this forest in the shape of a bear so that he might rob me of my treasure. Now I am free and able to return to my father's palace."

"Will – will you not return first to our cottage?" said Snow-White shyly. "Our mother would love to see you."

"Most certainly," said the young Prince, "for there is something very important that I must ask her."

Can you guess what it was? The Prince had long ago fallen in love with the gentle Snow-White and wished to ask her mother for permission to make her his wife. Of course this was gladly given. And after they were happily married, Snow-White told her sister and mother that she wanted them to live with her in the splendid palace. This they gladly consented to do, and great was the mother's joy when the Prince himself planted two rose trees in the royal gardens, one white and the other red, just like the ones that had once bloomed in her tiny cottage garden.

The Prince and the Emperor's Daughter

THERE WAS once a Prince who had a very small kingdom. This meant that for a Prince he was very poor. After a time he made up his mind to marry and being exceedingly handsome there were quite a number of pretty Princesses who would like to have been his wife. None, however, was as pretty as the Emperor's only daughter.

Now the Prince was too poor to send costly gifts to the Emperor's palace. But he said to himself, "I will send the two things I value most in the world. My precious rose bush and my own singing nightingale."

The rose bush bloomed only once in five years and whoever smelled the scent of the single red rose became instantly happy. The nightingale sang the sweetest melody of songs in all the world and those who heard it thought they were in heaven.

Certain that the Emperor's daughter would welcome these two wonderful gifts, the Prince put them in silver boxes and addressed them to the Princess.

The day they arrived, the Emperor himself received them and took them into the marble hall where the Princess was playing cards with her maids of honor. When she saw the boxes, she clapped her hands.

"I hope there is a little white pussy cat in one," she cried, "and a long-eared puppy in the other."

But, oh dear me, when the first silver box was opened, there was a rose bush with a single red rose.

All the court ladies said how pretty the rose was and what a wonderful perfume it had. But the Princess would scarcely look at it. "It it real?" she asked.

"Indeed it is," said one of her maids of honor. "It is the most beautiful rose I have ever seen."

"Take it away at once," stormed the Princess, stamping her tiny foot in its embroidered slipper. "I hate real flowers; their petals fall off and they die. It's a horrible present."

The Emperor looked at his daughter sadly. "How spoiled she is," he thought. "All her life she has had everything she asked for and now nothing pleases her." Then he opened the second box.

The little brown nightingale began at once to sing its charming melody of songs as the Emperor placed its silver cage on the table.

"Beautiful! Quite entrancing!" cried the court ladies, as they listened.

But the spoiled Princess asked, "Is it a mechanical bird – one I can wind up when I want to?"

"No, no, it is a real bird," her youngest maid of honor told her. "And that makes it all the more wonderful. Who would want a toy nightingale instead of a real one, particularly when it sings like this?"

"I would!" cried the Princess, stamping her foot once again. "I don't want it and I won't have it." And she picked up the silver cage and ran to the window.

"Let me have it please," said the youngest maid of honor, who was also the boldest. But the Princess opened the cage and threw the bird into the air. "Go back to your master," she called after it, as it flew away. "Tell him that should he dare to come to my father's palace, I most certainly will not see him."

News of how the Princess had received his precious gift was soon brought to the Prince. "If the Princess will not see me as I am," he said, "I will go to the palace disguised as a swineherd."

So the Prince stained his face brown and black, put on shabby, patched clothes and pulled a battered old hat down over his face. Then off he went to the Emperor's palace. "It happens that we do need a swineherd to take care of the pigs," said the head steward, when the

Prince spoke to him in the imperial gardens. "The job is yours if you care to take it."

"I'll do my best," said the false swineherd.

So the Prince was appointed the Emperor's swineherd. He was given a miserable hut to sleep in and a hundred pigs to look after. The work was hard and dirty but the new swineherd went about it cheerfully and in his spare time he would sit outside his hut making a little pot with bells all around it. When it was finished, he built a small fire, and placed the pot on top. Then he filled it with water. As soon as the water began to boil the bells rang out in a very pretty way and played an old tune.

Now one day the Princess was out walking with her maids of honor. Suddenly she heard the sound of one of her favorite tunes and it sounded so pretty that she sent one of her court ladies to the swineherd to ask for the pot.

"Ask him how much he wants for it," she said. "Tell him the Princess desires to have it."

The court lady was soon back. "I scarcely dare to tell you what the impudent wretch said," she confessed, almost in tears. "He will not sell his pot for money. He wants ten kisses from you."

The Princess was so surprised that she forgot to show the anger which would have been proper in a true lady.

"What a rude fellow that swineherd must be!" she said, at last. "Of course, a Princess should not think of such things . . ." She broke off, as the pot once again began to tinkle merrily. "But, well, yes I will give him ten kisses if that is the only way I can get the pot."

So the proud, spoiled Princess went to the swineherd and all her maids of honor stood around the pair so that no passerby would see the Emperor's daughter kissing a swineherd.

The very next week the Princess came across the swineherd once again. He had made a rattle that played all the waltzes and polkas and merry jigs imaginable whenever he swung it. As he walked along he swung his rattle and the music it made set the court ladies, accompanying the Princess, dancing and hopping.

"I'll have that rattle," said the Princess, whose own dainty little feet were tapping the ground. "It will amuse me in the evenings and is much better than any of my music boxes."

"Shall I ask him what he wants for it?" whispered the youngest maid of honor.

"Yes, do that," said the Princess.

The youngest maid of honor came back to her mistress with flushed cheeks and bright eyes. "I do not know how to tell you what he said," she confessed. "Something dreadful! He says you must give him one hundred kisses for the musical rattle."

"Indeed I will not,"said the Princess. "The impudent fellow has

gone too far.'' But as she spoke the swineherd swung his rattle and all her maids of honor began jigging up and down in time to its merry tune. ''Yet it is truly a marvelous rattle,'' she went on. ''Yes, I will pay the price. But all of you must gather around and spread out your skirts so that no one sees the Emperor's daughter kissing her father's pig-man.''

Then the Princess went up to the swineherd and all the ladies of the court gathered around the pair and spread out their dresses.

Meanwhile, as the Princess began kissing the swineherd who was really a Prince, her father stepped out on the balcony. He rubbed his eyes and put on his spectacles. ''Now what are those maids of honor up to?'' he asked himself. ''What new tricks are they playing?''

And he pushed his feet firmly into his slippers and hurried down to the courtyard. He hurried so much that he was quite out of breath, but in his soft slippers he made no sound and the maids of honor were too busy counting the kisses to notice him.

Then the Emperor stood on tip-toe and was so shocked at what he saw that he took off one of his slippers and began hitting the court ladies on the head. ''Be off with you!'' he shouted, for he was very angry. ''Be off with you!''

Then the Emperor saw what he must do if he were to bring his daughter to her senses. ''I forbid you to return to the palace,'' he said. ''You are not fit to be a Princess.''

Of course the swineherd, too, was sent away. And outside the palace gates, he began to scold the spoiled Princess, telling her that he had lost a good job all because of her. And the Princess began to weep and wish that she had never been born.

''Oh, how silly I am,'' she sobbed. ''I could have married a handsome Prince but I wouldn't even see him because he sent me stupid presents.''

The swineherd left her sitting under a tree, crying her eyes out in the rain. Quickly he returned to his hut, washed the brown stain off his face and threw away his rags. Then he dressed himself in a fine velvet suit and looking every inch a royal Prince, even though his kingdom was very small, he returned to the weeping Princess.

At the sight of the tall handsome young man, the Princess dried her eyes and began to smile. ''I don't know who you are,'' she said, ''but you look like a Prince and I hope you will take me to your palace.''

''That I will never do,'' said the Prince. ''You would not accept my gifts. You did not value the rose and the nightingale that I sent you. You would not even see me. Yet, for a pot with bells on it and a

musical rattle, you were quite willing to kiss a swineherd. I was that swineherd and now I know that you are the most spoiled Princess in the whole world.''

Then the Prince went back to his own very small kingdom and, in time, he married a Princess who was just as pretty as the Emperor's daughter and not in the least bit spoiled.

The Crystal Ball

ONCE UPON a time a King decided to build a country house in some woods within his kingdom. But in these woods lived a wicked enchantress. Foresters came to the woods and cut down mighty trees. When she saw the King's foresters fell the mighty trees so they crashed to the ground, the enchantress was enraged. She became determined to seek revenge.

She waited quietly until one day two of the King's sons came to the wood to watch the house being built. Then the enchantress seized her chance and changed one of the sons into a great eagle doomed to

live in the high rocky mountains. The other son she changed into a giant whale whose home would henceforth be the vast ocean.

Satisfied that she had done the King great harm, the enchantress disappeared forever from the woods. But when news of the fate of his two sons reached the King's ears, he became ill with grief. After all, his third and youngest son was a gay, light-hearted fellow who was never serious for long. How could the King expect him to wear his crown when he grew too old to rule?

"Do not grieve so much, Father," said the young Prince, when he saw what was in the King's mind. "I will leave the palace and search for a magician whose power is great enough to restore my two brothers to their human shapes."

The King had little faith in his youngest son but he said nothing and gave his permission. The Prince set out at once. For many months he wandered the earth until at last he came to a land where the sun shone both day and night and where everything – the grass, the trees and the flowers – was a golden yellow.

"You are in the Land of the Golden Sun," an old man told him, as he sat down to rest on the edge of a deep forest.

"Do you have any magicians in this wonderful land?" asked the Prince.

"There is one," said the old man. "But he is both wicked and spiteful. Already he has carried off our King's only child, a lovely Princess. Now he holds her captive in a castle among the mountains."

"I will find that castle," cried the young Prince. "I will find it even if it takes me years and years and even if I grow old like you, Grandfather, in my search."

"Many young men as brave and handsome as yourself have tried," the old man warned him. "And none have returned."

The Prince waved and smiled cheerfully as he thanked the old man and set off through the forest. By and by he heard loud grunts and bellows, and he grasped his sword fearing that some wild animal was about to attack him. Instead, he came upon two huge giants with arms like tree trunks, engaged in a battle to the death. So fiercely were they fighting that the Prince saw that soon one or other of them would be killed.

"Stop!" he shouted at the top of his voice. "Surely there is another way to settle your quarrel!"

The giants paused and looked at him in astonishment. "Go away, little man," the red-haired giant roared.

27

"Not until you tell me what you are fighting about," answered the young Prince firmly.

The smaller of the giants, who had black hair down to his shoulders, pointed to a ragged old cap lying on the grass.

"We're fighting over the cap," he said. "Whoever wins will have it."

"You are surely joking!" exclaimed the Prince in surprise. "That shabby old cap is certainly not worth fighting over."

"Ah!" said the red-haired giant. "That's where you are wrong. It's a wishing-cap and whoever wears it can wish himself away to wherever he likes."

"Well, that does make it a bit special," said the Prince. "I tell you what – I'll put the cap on and go and stand under that great oak tree over there. Then you two must race towards me. Whoever wins the race wins the cap."

The two giants looked at each other. They were both tired of fighting and it seemed to them a sensible way to settle the argument. "We agree," said the red-haired giant. "Put on the wishing-cap and stand under the tree. We'll line up here and when you shout 'Go!' we'll race towards you."

The Prince picked up the cap, put it on his head and walked slowly towards the tree. But as he walked along, he began to think of his brothers and then of the beautiful Princess who was a prisoner in a castle which somehow he must find. And, without thinking, he sighed, "I wish I was in that magician's castle right now."

No one was more surprised than the Prince himself when he found he was standing on top of a high mountain before the gates of a castle that glinted and shimmered in the sun. Then he remembered the wishing-cap which was, of course, still on his head. "I cannot refuse this piece of good fortune," he thought. "But when I have found this spiteful magician and rescued the Princess, I will see to it that the giants have their wishing-cap back."

The Prince entered the castle, boldly determined to fight his way to the beautiful Princess. But every room he entered was empty. At last, at the end of a long passage, he came upon a small room and there inside stood – not the lovely Princess he was expecting – but a bent and shriveled old woman with a gray wrinkled face and thin brown hair that hung about her face like rats' tails.

Scarcely able to gaze upon such ugliness, the Prince was about to turn away, when the woman cried, "Do not go until you have seen what I really look like." And she ran to him, holding up a small silver-

backed mirror. "Look in the mirror!" she went on. "And you will see a Princess."

Obediently the Prince looked into the mirror and the face he saw there was so sweet and lovely that this time he could scarcely take his eyes away.

"I am under the spell of a wicked magician who lives in the tower of this castle," the Princess told him. "Alas, if you are determined to save me, there are many deeds of courage to be performed. Others who have reached the castle have perished in the attempt. I fear for your life, noble Prince."

"I am ready to do anything," replied the Prince, keeping his eyes firmly fixed on the mirror. "Only tell me what I must do to free you from this terrible spell."

"You must find the crystal ball," the Princess told him. "But first you must leave this castle and take on, in mortal combat, a mighty wild bull. It will toss you on its terrible horns and dash you to the ground unless you find the way straight to its heart with your sword."

"I will fight this wild bull and I will kill it," promised the Prince.

"When it lies dead at your feet," continued the Princess, "a fiery bird will spring out of it. This fiery bird will hold in its claws a large, round egg which is red-hot to the touch. Inside this burning egg is the crystal ball. When you have the crystal ball the magician can work no evil against you. Instead he will be in your power and ready to carry out your commands."

"There are but three things I desire most in life," said the Prince. "I must restore my poor brothers to their human shapes, and I must break the spell which holds you . . ." Then he smiled. "Do not ask me the third. There will be time enough to tell you when all else is accomplished."

Then the brave young Prince, with drawn sword, ran from the castle and down the mountainside. There, at the bottom, a wild bull with long cruel horns waited to do battle with him. Many times the Prince tried to drive his sword into the bull's heart and many times he failed. Once he was tossed high into the air by the bull's terrible horns and once he was almost trampled into the ground by its flashing hooves. But always the Prince returned to the battle.

31

And at last, after a long and desperate struggle, he plunged his sword deep into the beast's heart. As the mighty animal slowly sank to the ground, a great fiery bird rose from its body and flew upwards into the sky. Watching it helplessly, the Prince saw that it held a huge round red egg in its powerful claws.

In dismay the Prince threw himself down to the ground. Despite the terrible battle he had, after all, lost everything, for he knew that inside the egg lay the crystal ball.

Suddenly, as he looked despairingly upwards, there soared through the sky a huge eagle. The Prince felt his heart begin to beat faster. He knew the mighty eagle was his brother, and he was going to challenge the fiery bird. The eagle swooped down upon the bird, driving it out to sea and striking it time and again with its powerful beak until at last the bird dropped its precious egg into the sea.

"Alas," thought the Prince as he ran to the water's edge. "It has all been in vain, for now the egg is lost at the bottom of the sea." But, how wrong he was! The egg suddenly appeared in a tall jet of water! Then the Prince saw the enormous whale, spouting water, and knew that his second brother had come to his rescue.

The whale cast the egg on to the sandy beach where it lay, red, but no longer burning-hot. The Prince picked it up and cracked it open. There inside was the crystal ball.

Shouting for joy, the Prince ran up the mountainside and into the castle. Up, up a hundred narrow winding stairs he ran until he reached the magician's tower. There he found the magician, crouching over a crystal ball which was clouded and misted over. The magician did not look at the Prince as he burst into the room. But he muttered, "You are lord of the castle, and master of the magicians, now. What do you want?"

"If I am all these things," said the Prince, holding out his crystal ball to the magician, "then I can restore my brothers to their true shape and the Princess to her former beauty."

"It is done, master," said the magician. "Look into your crystal ball."

The Prince stared into his crystal ball and to his great joy and happiness he saw his two brothers walking, arm-in-arm, in his father's courtyard. Then he saw the Princess, her blonde hair falling like gold silk over her slender shoulders, and she was smiling as she gazed into her mirror.

"I want nothing more from you," he told the magician. "Leave the castle immediately and I will not try to punish you for your wicked deeds."

In answer, the magician rose to his feet, and with a fading wail, he vanished in a cloud of dust before the astonished Prince had time to cry out.

The lovely Princess was waiting for him as he ran from the tower, down, down the winding stairs and into her room.

"What is the third desire you spoke of?" she asked shyly, as he took her in his arms.

"To ask you to marry me," the Prince laughed. "And to take you back to my father's palace where your beauty and sweetness will win all hearts."

So the Prince and the Princess were married and in time a beautiful baby girl was born to them. And when she was old enough they told her the story of the crystal ball that always sat on a red velvet cushion in a silver box in the throne room.

"I like it when the two giants were fighting," said the little girl. "What happened to the wishing-cap?"

Then the Prince lifted the magic crystal ball from its silver box and asked her to look into it. And what do you think she saw? She saw the shabby old wishing-cap hanging from the branch of a tree and beside it, two mighty giants, one red-haired and the other black-haired, wrestling fiercely.

"Perhaps you should have kept the wishing-cap, after all," said the little Princess wisely. "Then they wouldn't have anything to fight about!"

What do you think?

The Garden of Paradise

ONCE UPON a time there was a King's son who, when he was very young, loved listening to stories. His grandmother told him the best stories of all and the one he liked to hear over and over again was about the Garden of Paradise.

"The Garden of Paradise," she would say, "is the most beautiful place you can imagine. Every flower is a delicious little cake and on some, the history of the world is written. You have only to eat one of these little cakes and you know your history lesson from A to Z."

At the time, the small boy believed this. But as he grew older, he heard about Adam and Eve, the man and woman who first lived in the Garden of Paradise, and he understood that it was not exactly as his grandmother had described.

As he grew older the King's son loved books more than anything and by the time he was seventeen he had a huge library of splendid books. Day after day he searched in them for mention of the Garden of Paradise but although they told him many things about the world, they said nothing of the Garden which filled all his thoughts.

One day, as he walked alone in the forest, the sky suddenly grew dark with heavy black clouds. Then it began to rain so heavily that it poured down on him like a great river, soaking him through and

through. The Prince had wandered away from the familiar paths and by nightfall he was lost. Stumbling and slipping over the moss-covered stones and faint with weariness and hunger, he came at last upon an enormous cave.

In the middle of this cave a huge fire burned and there, on a spit, was a big stag slowly turning around and around. Beside the fire sat a woman, so tall and strong that it seemed to the young Prince she could have been a man. When she saw him, she called out, "Come nearer. Come and sit by the fire and dry your clothes."

"Thank you," said the Prince, and he entered the cave and sat down beside her on the ground. "When the storm came so suddenly I lost my way in the forest."

"You are now in the Cavern of the Winds," said the woman, as she threw some logs on the fire. "I am the mother of the Four Winds. They will be home presently."

"What do they do, these four sons of yours?" asked the Prince curiously.

"They are in business on their own account up there with the clouds," the woman answered gruffly, and once again the Prince thought how different she was from any of the women at his father's court.

As if reading his thoughts, the woman went on, "You do not understand. I am their mother and I must be strong to keep them in order for my sons are wild fellows. Do you see those four sacks hanging on the wall?"

The Prince looked at the big sacks and nodded. "I saw them at once," he said, "as soon as I came into the cave."

"My sons are afraid of those sacks," laughed the mother of the Four Winds. "When they do wrong I bend them and pop them into the sacks. There they must stay until I choose to let them out. They know well enough what will happen to them if they disobey me or anger me."

"When will your sons return?" asked the Prince, after a long silence.

"Here comes one now," she cried, as there was a sudden rush of icy cold wind. "Here he is. Here is my eldest, the North Wind."

The Prince shivered with cold as the North Wind came into the cave. What a huge fellow he was, dressed in bears' skins and with long icicles hanging from his beard. His cap and boots were of sealskin and he was covered with snowflakes.

"Don't go too near the fire," the Prince cried out in alarm. "You'll get frost-bite!"

But the giant North Wind only laughed, a deep, bellowing roar, as he looked down at the Prince. "What's this mannikin doing here?" he asked his mother.

"He lost his way," his mother told him, "and now he is my guest. If you do not treat him kindly you will have to go into the sack."

And she threw more wood on the fire. "Now tell us where you have been."

"I've been to the Polar Seas," said the North Wind, no longer laughing, at the mention of the sack. "I've been to Bear's Island with the walrus hunters. I blew away the mist that hung over the hunters' house that they had built of ship-wrecked wood and covered with walrus skins. And I teased the polar bear that growled at me. Then I blew my ships, the great icebergs, until they crushed the tiny man-made boats in which sat the men-harpoonists. I covered them with snowflakes and drove them out to sea. They won't come near Bear's Island again."

"That was a wicked thing to do," scolded his mother. "I'll hear no more of your story."

"I'll say no more then," replied the North Wind, glancing nervously at the sacks. "Here comes my little brother from the west."

The Prince thought the West Wind looked like a wild man of the forests as he rushed into the cavern carrying a heavy club and wearing a broad-brimmed hat that came down over his eyes. His mother smiled at him and asked him where he had been.

"I've come from the green forests," he said, "where the water snakes lie in the wet grass and the wild buffalo swim in the rivers. I chased the wild ducks and I blew a storm so that the old trees crashed down and broke into splinters. I really enjoyed myself today."

Presently, as they talked, the South Wind arrived. He wore a turban on his head and a flowing cloak around his shoulders which reminded the Prince of pictures of desert travelers he had seen in his books at home.

"How cold it is in here," cried the South Wind, and he threw more wood on the fire. "That's my big brother's fault."

"Nonsense," said the North Wind. "It's so hot in here you could roast a polar bear."

"Stop!" ordered their mother, pointing to the sacks. "I want to hear your story, South Wind. Where have you come from?"

"Africa," said the South Wind. "I ran races with the ostriches and when I came to the desert I met a caravan. The people were just about to kill their last camel to get water. So I blew the soft yellow sand into whirling pillars and I covered them all, camel and caravan, with the sand. It was fun. One day I'll go back and blow the sand away and take a look at their white bones. . ."

"Wicked fellow!" cried his mother angrily. "You have done nothing but evil." And she seized the South Wind around the body and popped him into one of the sacks, before he could utter a sound.

"Your sons certainly are wild men," remarked the young Prince. "What of the East Wind? Is he like his brothers?"

"You may judge for yourself," said the mother of the Winds softly, as the East Wind entered the cavern.

The Prince saw that the East Wind was shorter than his brothers and that he was dressed like a man from China.

39

"So you have been in China," said his mother fondly. "I thought you were going to the Garden of Paradise."

"I fly there tomorrow," said the East Wind. "It will be a hundred years tomorrow since I was last there. In China I had only time to whistle through the bamboo forests and ring all the bells in the big cities. But it was fun!"

"You are foolish," said the old woman. "I am glad you are going to the Garden of Paradise tomorrow. You may learn some sense. Bring me home a small bottle filled with the water from the Spring of Wisdom."

"I will," said the East Wind. "But let my brother, the South Wind, come out of the sack. He must tell another story about the Phœnix bird so that I can tell it to the Fairy Queen in the Garden of Paradise. She always wants to hear about the Phœnix bird."

"Very well," said his mother. "I love you best of all and it's hard to refuse you anything."

The Prince smiled when he saw the South Wind creep out of the sack like a naughty schoolboy. "I can tell you about the Phœnix bird," he said. "I have read about him in some of my books at home. He came out of an egg that lay in a burning nest. It was red hot because his mother had set herself and the nest on fire."

"You are right," said the South Wind. "There is only one Phœnix bird left in the world. The last time I met him he gave me this palm leaf for the Princess."

"She will like that," said the East Wind, taking the leaf.

The Prince stared at the East Wind with eager interest. "Tell me about the Garden of Paradise," he cried. "Where does it lie?"

"Do you want to go there?" asked the East Wind, as he began to eat some of the roasted deer his mother gave him.

"With all my heart," answered the Prince.

"You have heard of Adam and Eve, I suppose," continued the East Wind. "Well, when they were driven out of the Garden, it sank into the earth. It is still wonderfully beautiful but now the Queen of the Fairies lives there. Sit on my back tomorrow and I will take you there if you wish."

After their supper, the brothers lay down to sleep and the Prince lay down beside them. Soon he, too, was fast asleep. When he next opened his eyes, it was early morning and to his surprise he found that he was sitting on the East Wind's back and flying high above the clouds. If the East Wind had not been holding on to his arms, he would almost certainly have toppled off.

"You didn't give me a chance to thank your mother or say farewell to your brothers," said the Prince at last. "I am sorry about that."

"I wanted to make an early start," said the East Wind. "We have a very long way to go before we reach the Garden of Paradise." And he flew on and on, over forests and high mountains and across vast seas.

As it grew dark, the East Wind said, "Hold tight, for now we are coming to the highest mountains in the world. Then soon we shall come to the Garden of Paradise."

"I'm glad to hear it," said the Prince, who was tired of hanging on. "It seems that the air is beginning to smell more sweetly as if it were scented with flowers and spices."

"You're right," the East Wind told him. "We are now quite close

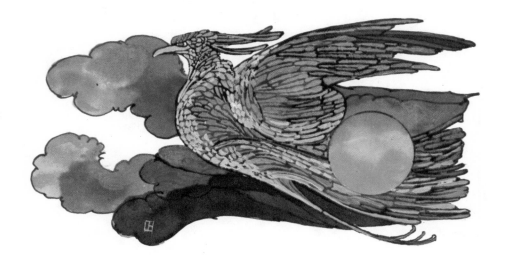

to the Garden." And he began to drop out of the sky, flying lower and lower until at last he landed on soft green grass. The Prince jumped off his back and stretched himself thankfully.

"How beautiful it is!" he exclaimed. "The grass is so green and the flowers all the colors of the rainbow."

"We have not yet arrived at the Garden," said the East Wind. "We must pass through that huge cave you see there in front of you where the vines hang like green curtains. That is the way to the Garden of Paradise."

What a strange cave it was! To begin with the Prince found it icy cold and he began to shiver violently. A few steps later and it was warm, bathed in brilliant sunshine. Great blocks of stones, curiously shaped, stood along the walls of the cavern and sometimes the passage was so narrow that the Prince had to squeeze and push his way forward. Then, at last, he saw just ahead of him the most wonderful blue sky.

The air was filled with the scent of roses as the Prince left the cavern and came to a halt beside a clear river where little fishes, silver and gold, flashed in and out among colored stones that glistened like jewels. A marble bridge spanned this river and the East Wind led him across. "We are now on the Island of Happiness," said he, "where the Garden of Paradise lies."

"How wonderful!" cried the Prince, "Everything is so much more

beautiful than I ever imagined." And he smiled with pleasure as he looked about him and saw the strange delicate flowers, the climbing plants and green vines.

A flock of peacocks, their trains spread out like brilliant fans, walked towards him. And then he saw among the trees, antelopes and tigers, so tame that the wild wood pigeons were perching on their backs. Scarcely able to breathe for wonder and happiness, the Prince lost all count of time.

Presently, as he stood there, the Fairy Queen of Paradise appeared. She was young and very beautiful with a star in her long golden hair. The East Wind greeted her like a friend and he gave her the palm leaf from the Phoenix bird. Then he turned to the Prince. "He is a friend of mine," he smiled. "Will you take care of him?"

And the Fairy took the Prince's hand and led him into her palace. In the middle of the vast marble hall where the Prince found himself, he saw a tree, tall and straight, and heavy with shining golden apples.

"Is this the Tree of Knowledge?" he asked, knowing that it must be, and the Fairy Queen nodded and smiled.

"Can – can I always stay here?" he asked, his eyes bright with happiness. "It is what I desire most in the world!"

"That depends on yourself," answered the Fairy. "You must do what I tell you. If you disobey, all will be lost."

"I will be strong," cried the Prince. "I will take nothing that is forbidden."

"The East Wind leaves tonight," said the Fairy. "He will not return for a hundred years. That is a long time to wait."

"It will pass quickly," said the Prince. "Please let me stay."

"If you do," replied the Fairy, "every evening when I leave you I shall have to call to you, 'Come with me.' But you must not obey. You must stay where you are."

"I understand," the Prince said eagerly. "I promise I will not try to follow you."

"I will do all in my power to persuade you to come to me," said the Fairy Queen. "If you do follow me, you will find me under the Tree of Knowledge. Bend down and kiss me and the Garden of Paradise will sink into the earth and be lost to you forever."

"I promise I will not come to you," declared the Prince. "No matter how often you call me."

Then the East Wind appeared and said, "We shall meet here in a hundred years. Take good care of yourself." And he spread out his broad wings and flew away.

For the rest of that wonderful day the beautiful Fairy Queen stayed with the Prince, dancing with him among the flowers, and sitting beside him under the green trees. When the sun went down, she led him into a room filled with white and golden lilies and some of her maidens brought him fruit to eat and wine to drink.

"Now," said she, "it is time for me to leave you." But as she left the room, the Prince could hear her gentle voice calling, "Come with me! Come with me!" And forgetting his promise, he rushed after her.

When he came to the great hall where the Tree of Knowledge stood, he saw her, lying on a bed of leaves, under its spreading branches. And, although her eyes were closed as if in sleep, she was smiling. She was so beautiful that the Prince could not stop himself from bending down and kissing her.

Immediately there was a fearful clap of thunder – so loud and terrifying that the Prince fell to the ground in terror, his eyes closed. When next he opened them, a cold rain was beating down on his face and he was shivering as if he had a fever. He struggled to his feet and saw that he was in the forest close to the Cavern of the Winds. Then he saw the mother of the Winds and she looked at him fiercely. "You

have failed," she said. "And on your very first evening! If you were a son of mine I would put you into the sack!"

"Yes, I have failed," said the Prince sadly. "I have lost everything. Shall I ever get a second chance?"

"Who knows?" said the mother of the Winds. And she went into the cave, leaving him alone in the forest.

What do you think happened to the Prince? Some say he wandered the world for a hundred years searching for the Garden of Paradise which he could never find. But others say that the East Wind took pity on him and carried him there on his back so that, after all, he could have a second chance.

Puss-in-Boots

THERE WAS once a poor miller who had three sons. He was so poor that when he died he left only his mill, his donkey and his cat.

"I'll take the mill," said the eldest son. "The mill is mine by rights."

"I'll take the donkey," said the second son. "With the donkey to carry loads, I can set up in business on my own."

"That leaves me with the cat," said the third and youngest son. "How is a cat going to help me to earn my living? What am I going to do?"

His two brothers were much too greedy and selfish to care, so the miller's youngest son took the cat and went off by himself to think out what he could do.

"I shall almost certainly starve to death," he said aloud, as he sat down under a tree. "Life is very unfair."

"I wouldn't say that," remarked the cat. "You could find me of great use if you would only trust me."

"What! Trust a cat to make my fortune," exclaimed the young man scornfully. "That's a very fine thing to ask me to do."

Now it didn't seem a bit strange to the miller's son that he should find himself talking to a cat. At the time of which I write, there were quite a few talking animals around and the miller's son knew this. Besides he couldn't help remembering that his father's cat had been quite exceptionally clever in the way he had caught rats and mice.

"All I need," said the cat, after a short silence, "is a pair of high boots and a big sack. Give them to me and I promise that you will not be disappointed."

In spite of himself, the miller's youngest son began to believe in his cat. "I have very little money left," he said. "But I am willing to spend it on high boots for you although, I must admit, I cannot see why you want them. As for the sack, that is easily found."

"Never mind why I want the boots," said the cat. "Just wait and see."

As soon as the cat put on his fine new pair of red boots he seemed to grow more important, more certain of what he was going to do. "You wait here," he told his young master. "I'm going into the woods with my sack."

Puss-in-Boots wasted no time in the woods. First he filled his sack with bran and lettuce. Then he looped a long string around the neck of the sack so that he could close it whenever he wished. When this was done to his satisfaction, he lay down, the string in his paw, and pretended to be dead.

Now it is a well known fact that rabbits are very fond of lettuce and bran and, before long, a plump young rabbit hopped up to the sack. It smelled the bran and caught a glimpse of the tempting lettuce. Puss held the string firmly as the silly rabbit hopped inside the sack. And that was the end of the foolish young rabbit! Puss pulled the string, closed the sack's neck and pounced on his prisoner.

Well satisfied with his morning's work, Puss-in-Boots set off at once for the King's palace. So important did he look in his shining high boots that he was taken straightaway to the King.

"A gift, Your Majesty," said Puss-in-Boots, without wasting words. "A gift from my most gracious and noble master, the Marquis of Carabas." This was the grand-sounding name that Puss had invented for the miller's son as he left the woods.

Now the King, as Puss knew, was extremely fond of rabbit pie and when he saw the plump young rabbit, he could hardly hide his royal pleasure. He coughed and his eyes twinkled. "Ahem!" he said at last, knowing that a king should not appear too pleased at receiving a present. "I am very grateful to your master, the – ahem – the Marquis of . . ."

"Carabas," said Puss firmly. "The Marquis of Carabas."

"Indeed yes," said the King. "The Marquis of Carabas. Yes, well, I shall certainly remember that name."

Puss-in-Boots, in fact, gave the King no chance to forget it for the very next morning he turned up at the palace with a pair of very fine wood pigeons; and the day after, with a plump pheasant.

By the end of the week, the King had eaten rabbit and pigeon pie to his heart's content and had almost begun to think of the Marquis of Carabas as a friend.

"I must meet your master soon," he said to Puss, when next the cat visited the palace. "I should very much like to thank him in person for so many fine gifts."

This was all Puss-in-Boots had been waiting to hear. He ran straight back to his master who, by this time, was extremely dirty and shabby though he always ate well, thanks to Puss.

"You must bathe in the river tomorrow at a certain hour," Puss told the young man. "Just do as I say and all will be well."

"I don't see why I should," grumbled the miller's son. "The water is cold at this time of the year and besides I have never enjoyed swimming."

"Never mind that," said Puss briskly. "I'll show you the exact spot where you must enter the river when the time comes."

By now, of course, the miller's son knew that Puss-in-Boots was up to something and could only hope that plans were underway to make his fortune. "Very well," he agreed. "I'll do what you ask."

The next morning Puss took his master to a spot on the riverside which was not far from the road. Only the week before Puss-in-Boots had learned from some of the palace servants that the King and his charming daughter were in the habit of driving along this road in their carriage, and he had made his plans accordingly.

As soon as his master was undressed, Puss hid the ragged bundle of clothes under a big stone. Then he pushed him into the water. And then, down the road at a fine rattling pace came the King's carriage, and Puss began to shout at the top of his voice, "Help! Help! My master, the Marquis of Carabas, is drowning!"

So loudly and desperately did Puss shout that the King's attention was immediately attracted. "Stop!" he called to his coachman. "I know that name!" Then he saw Puss-in-Boots, and the cat pointed to the young man in midstream.

"My coachman will have him out of the water in a trice," the King assured Puss.

As the coachman somewhat unwillingly went to the rescue, Puss hastily whispered in the King's ear. "All my master's beautiful clothes

have been stolen," he told him. "Could you possibly have a new suit sent from the palace?"

"Yes indeed!" declared the King. "That is the least I can do."

When the miller's son was finally dressed in one of the King's own suits he looked very handsome indeed. So handsome, in fact, that the Princess, who had sat silent for all this time, gave him a very gracious smile and invited him to join her in the royal carriage.

"This is the noble Marquis of Carabas, my dear," said the King, as he too settled himself in the carriage. "He has sent us many fine gifts over the past weeks."

The miller's son heard this with great astonishment but was clever

enough to hide his surprise. Besides, the Princess was so very lovely that he just wanted to sit close to her forever.

Meanwhile, Puss was speeding down the road in his high boots. Soon he was ahead of the King's carriage and when he came upon some peasants working in a rich, golden meadow he stopped.

"Listen, my good fellows," he shouted. "In a few minutes the King's carriage will pass this way. If you do not tell him that this rich meadow and all the land surrounding it belongs to the Marquis of Carabas, I will have you chopped into little pieces . . ."

Puss-in-Boots looked and sounded so fierce that the peasants touched their caps and said, "We'll do as you say."

With a final scowl and a warning, Puss sped on his way for already he could hear the sound of horses' hooves behind him. Almost before he had rounded the next bend in the road, the King's carriage had reached the meadow.

Now the King was a greedy King and the sight of such a splendid golden meadow made him curious as to its owner.

"The Marquis of Carabas owns this meadow and all the land surrounding it," the peasants said in answer to the King's question.

"Indeed!" exclaimed the King, and he smiled in a very friendly way at the miller's son.

Running as fast as he could, Puss was able to keep ahead of the royal carriage. Whenever he saw a particularly rich field of crops or a well wooded piece of land he stopped. He always said the same thing to the peasants working close by.

"If you do not tell the King that all this land belongs to the Marquis of Carabas," he warned, "I will have you chopped into little pieces . . ."

In this way, clever Puss made certain that the King would soon

think that his master was one of the richest young men in his kingdom. But there was still more work to be done. He must find a castle. The only castle Puss-in-Boots had heard about belonged to an ogre who was also a magician.

When Puss reached the ogre's castle, he found him preparing for a banquet. "Well, what do you want?" demanded the ogre, in an unfriendly way.

"I have heard that you have marvelous powers," Puss said, bowing very low.

This pleased the ogre. "That's true," he admitted. "Marvelous powers – you never said a truer word."

"That's why I've come to see you," said Puss. "I – I just wanted to look at you."

"Well, that's a fine thing!" roared the ogre, suddenly very friendly. "That's what I call fame!"

"Of course you are famous, Sir Ogre," said Puss humbly. "You're so famous that I just had to pay you a visit. Do you know that some people say you can change yourself into any animal shape you choose?"

"So I can!" boasted the ogre. "You name the animal and I'll show you . . ."

"Even a lion?" asked Puss, his voice full of admiration.

"Even a lion!" roared the ogre, and, in a moment, Puss-in-Boots found himself face to face with a snarling lion. He got such a fright that he jumped, trembling, onto the window sill.

"That's – that's really wonderful, Sir Ogre," he squeaked. "But I suppose it's fairly easy for an ogre to change into such a huge creature as a lion?"

"It's no harder than changing into a tiger," said the ogre, when he was himself again.

"Ah, yes, well a tiger is much the same size as a lion," said Puss, jumping down from the sill. "But how about something really small – well, like a . . ." He stopped.

"I see what you mean!" laughed the ogre. "You think a big fellow like me can't make myself into a tiny creature, is that it?"

"Well, no, of course not," said Puss, but somehow he managed to look as if he didn't quite believe that the ogre could turn himself into something really small.

"You name the animal!" boasted the ogre, more than ever anxious to show off his powers.

"Well, the smallest creature I can think of is a mouse," said Puss.

"Watch!" cried the ogre, and with that he changed himself into a small brown mouse.

That was the moment Puss had been waiting for. With a snarl and a pounce he flattened the mouse on the floor and then ate it. That was the end of the ogre and certainly from Puss-in-Boot's point of view it happened not a moment too soon. He had only just time to rush up to the castle gates and be standing there as the royal carriage appeared.

"Upon my soul!" exclaimed the King. "There's Puss-in-Boots!"

"Welcome, Your Majesty, to the castle of my master the Marquis of Carabas," cried Puss, as the carriage stopped.

"So this splendid castle is yours!" exclaimed the King to the miller's son, as he helped the Princess to the ground. "Remarkably fine!"

The miller's son was by this time so deeply in love with the beautiful Princess that he was quite unable to say anything . . . which was just as well.

Puss-in-Boots led the small party into the banqueting room where the table was already, most fortunately, laid and the King's eyes sparkled at the sight of the gold plates and so many crystal goblets. "I don't know your feelings, young man," he said, turning to the miller's son. "But if, as it would seem, you have fallen in love with my daughter and wish to marry her, I won't stand in your way."

"If the Princess will have me," replied the miller's son, finding his tongue at last, "I shall be the happiest man in your kingdom."

"I will," cried the Princess, who was one of those girls who makes up her mind very quickly. "I haven't found anyone I like better."

So there and then, before they sat down at table, the wedding was arranged and there was no one more delighted than Puss himself.

After the wedding, which was held the very next day, Puss, at his own request, was given a new and exceedingly costly pair of high boots and a simply gorgeous outfit to match them.

In the eyes of his master, at least, nothing was too good for Puss-in-Boots!

The Little Mermaid

ONCE UPON a time there was a beautiful little mermaid. Her father was the Sea King and she lived with him and her five sisters in a wonderful palace in the deepest part of the ocean.

The Sea King's daughters were all very pretty but the prettiest of all was the youngest, the little mermaid whose skin was as fresh as rose petals and whose eyes were as blue as cornflowers.

The little mermaid was quieter than her sisters. Her playthings were the fishes with gold and silver scales that swam all day in and out of the castle. She did not enjoy visiting the shipwrecks as her sisters did and she was sad whenever a poor broken ship sank to the bottom of the sea. Whenever this happened she hid in the beautiful gardens that surrounded her father's castle. Here, among the red and dark blue flowers and the golden fruits, she dreamed of the moment she was longing for – the moment when she would be fifteen years old.

The reason that she longed for this time was that on her fifteenth birthday, every sea maiden was allowed to swim wherever she pleased. If she wanted to, she could rise to the surface of the sea and sit on the rocks or swim close to the shore where the earth people lived. Once, the little mermaid had found a boy statue with a gentle, handsome face that had come from a shipwreck. She had carefully carried the boy statue back with her to her own special part of the garden and it had become her dearest possession. It was because of the statue that she longed so much to see the earth people for herself.

At last the day came when the Sea King's youngest daughter was fifteen years old. Her wise old grandmother had told her much about the earth people, and now she would be able to see them for herself.

"You will find them strange," her grandmother told her, as they sat together on her birthday. "Our bodies end in graceful fishes' tails. They walk on two supports that are called legs."

"Then we can never be truly like them?" asked the mermaid.

"No," said her grandmother. "We cannot shed tears like the earth people and we do not look forward to another life above the heavens as they do. When we die we become foam on the waves of the sea. But we live much longer than they do – for three hundred years – and we have much to make us happy."

"I long to know the earth people," murmured the mermaid, but her grandmother pretended not to hear.

"You are the loveliest of the Sea King's daughters," the wise old mermaid went on. "And you have the most beautiful singing voice of all the sea maidens. You should be very happy."

Then her grandmother placed a garland of white flowers that were really priceless pearls on the Princess's golden hair, and on her long glistening tail she fastened eight large oysters.

"They hurt!" protested the mermaid.

"That does not matter," said her grandmother sternly. "The oysters are a sign of your rank. Those you meet on your travels will know that you are a daughter of a King when they see the oysters."

When she was quite ready, the Princess said goodbye to her family and her friends. Then she rose like a water-bubble up through the blue

sea. As she lifted her head above the waves, she could see the bright stars and the pale crimson of the sky. But more beautiful than the stars and sky was the great ship with three masts that rocked gently at its anchor nearby. The little mermaid had never before seen such a ship nor the sailors who sailed her.

There was music coming from the ship and as the night grew darker, hundreds of lanterns were lit and men and women, beautifully and richly dressed, crowded the deck. Presently the mermaid saw a young man appear, laughing merrily and holding a glass in his hand. Oh, how handsome he was and how he reminded her of the boy statue she kept in her garden at home. After a while, the little mermaid realized that the young man was a Prince and that today was his birthday.

Greatly daring, the little mermaid swam closer to the big ship, her long tail gleaming silver in the light from its lanterns. But almost at once she dived beneath the waves as a shower of golden rockets shot up into the sky and the sea was suddenly aglow with a thousand flashing stars.

When the party was over and the ship was quiet and dark, the mermaid knew that it was time for her to return to her father's palace.

But she could not bear to leave the ship, so she swam around and around, delaying her moment of departure. Presently she saw dark storm clouds gather in the sky. The wind, too, began to rise and the waves suddenly were like swirling black mountains.

Sailors rushed on deck, hurriedly pulling down the great sails and setting the ship on a course that carried her over the waves. But, alas, at the height of the terrible storm, the main masts broke and the proud ship rolled over on her side.

The little mermaid swam anxiously among the wooden beams and the casks that floated on the angry waves. No earth man could live in such a raging sea. If she did not find the Prince she knew he would drown and she could not – must not – allow this to happen. The Princess heard the despairing cries of the sailors but she thought only of the Prince and when at last she found him, he was already half drowned.

Holding his head above the water, she swam with him towards the shore and then, with all her strength, pulled him on to the smooth golden sand. For a time, the little mermaid cradled the young earth man in her arms, completely happy as she looked down at him. Then she slipped away, back into the sea, to wait and watch.

As the dawn appeared, she saw the Prince stir and soon some pretty young girls came down to the beach. At the sight of the Prince, one ran back to the town for help and, presently, the Prince was lifted on to a litter and carried away.

Sadly, the mermaid dived quickly under the water and returned to her father's castle. Almost at once she went to her own special garden to be near the boy statue that reminded her so much of her handsome Prince.

As the days passed, the little mermaid grew more and more thoughtful and quiet. She rarely smiled and she refused altogether to join in her sisters' merry antics and games.

"Tell us your secret," her eldest sister begged her one day. "Perhaps we can help you."

"You cannot help me," the little mermaid said. "I have fallen in love with an earth man, a tall handsome Prince."

"But we know where the Prince lives!" cried the eldest sister. "We have often seen him in his sailing boat. Come, we will take you to his palace."

Then the sisters linked arms and rose up together through the sparkling sea. "There!" cried the eldest, as they lifted their heads above the waves. "There is his palace; it comes almost down to the water's edge. We dare not swim too close but the Prince often comes and stands on the marble steps that lead into the water."

For the first time for many days, the little mermaid smiled happily. "Now, I can come here whenever I wish," she said. "I am content for I know that one day I shall see him again."

Every morning after that, the little mermaid rose up through the blue waters hoping to catch sight of the Prince. She swam closer to the land than any of her sisters would have dared and she came to know the fishermen and the times when the young Prince sailed his boat.

"How long do the earth people live?" the little mermaid asked her grandmother one day, as she combed out her golden hair.

"Not very long," said her grandmother. "But they do not die as we do. Why do you ask me again about such matters?"

"I do not want to become foam on the waves," said the Princess sadly. "I want to be like the earth people."

Her grandmother had no patience with such talk. "You are a sea maiden," she told the Princess sharply. "You have a fish-tail and you cannot expect to be accepted by the earth people. No earth man could ever love you because of your fish-tail – he would think it ugly."

That night the little mermaid sang more sweetly than ever for her father and her sisters. At the end of her song she slipped quietly away. Her mind was made up. She knew what she must do. She must visit the terrible sea-witch whose powers were known and feared throughout the sea kingdom.

No flowers grew where the sea-witch lived. There was nothing but deep dark whirlpools and the way was covered with black slimy mud. The sea-witch's house stood among tall twisting reeds that looked like fat yellow snakes. All around it were dangerous marshy swamps where only the poisonous creatures of the sea lived. So gloomy and terrifying was this place that the mermaid needed all her courage to swim towards the house.

She found the sea-witch sitting on a bench that was made out of the white bones of shipwrecked earth men. Snakes crawled over her arms and on her lap was her favorite pet, a fat ugly toad.

"I know what you want," said the sea-witch, as soon as the Princess swam up to her. "You want to get rid of your fish-tail and to have two supports so that the young earth Prince can fall in love with you."

"Yes, yes!" whispered the little mermaid. "That is what I want. Will you help me?"

"I will help you," said the sea-witch, "if you are willing to pay my price."

"I will pay it," said the Princess.

"Then I will prepare a magic potion which you must drink when you are on land," said the sea-witch. "Your tail will shrivel up and disappear and in its place you will have two legs. But there will be much pain. Are you willing to suffer?"

"Yes," whispered the mermaid.

"Whenever you walk it will be as if a sharp sword had pierced your feet," went on the witch. "But none will guess this for you will walk and dance with such grace that the eyes of the earth people will be dazzled by your beautiful movements."

"I am ready to endure the pain," said the mermaid. "What price must I pay for the gift of two legs?"

"You must give me your voice," said the witch. "It is the most beautiful voice in the sea kingdom, and I want it."

The Princess grew deathly pale. "But if I have no voice how can I tell the Prince of my love for him?" she asked quaveringly.

"Your eyes will tell him," said the sea-witch. "There will be no need for words. He will look into your eyes and see your love for him mirrored there."

"It is a high price," said the Princess at last, "but I am willing to pay it."

"So be it," said the witch. "But remember this. If you do not win the Prince's love and he marries someone else, your heart will break and you will, after all, become foam on the waves. You can never return to your father's castle."

"I understand," murmured the little mermaid. "I understand."

The witch brought out her black pot and began to make the potion that would change the mermaid into an earth girl. Many strange and horrible creatures she threw into the bubbling pot and the little mermaid covered her eyes so that she could not see the boiling mixture that steamed and hissed as the witch stirred and stirred. At last when the potion was ready, the witch dipped a small bottle into the pot and filled it with the liquid.

"There!" said the witch. "Take this bottle. Do not drink its contents until you are on land."

The mermaid took the bottle but she could not thank the witch for already her voice had gone. She was dumb.

Holding the bottle carefully, the little mermaid swam straight to the Prince's palace and dragged herself up on to the first step of the marble stairway where she had so often seen the Prince. Then she drank the witch's potion, draining the bottle to the very last drop.

It was just as the witch had said it would be. She felt terrible stabs of fearful pain as her fish-tail began to shrivel up. So great was the agony that the little mermaid could not bear it. She fainted. It was bright morning when she opened her eyes and saw the Prince himself standing over her. The Prince helped her up and the little mermaid, looking down, saw that she now had slim and white and very dainty little legs and feet.

The Prince was greatly taken with the little mermaid. He called her his little orphan from the sea, thinking that she had survived some shipwreck. When he found she could not speak, he petted her and made even more fuss of her, dressing her in pretty silk dresses and giving her golden slippers to wear on her tiny feet.

Soon, the little mermaid was everyone's favorite at court. When she danced, her movements were so graceful that they held the Prince spellbound. "Never have I seen such perfect dancing," he would say to her. And the little mermaid would look at him with eyes full of love, hiding the pain that pierced her feet like a sword whenever she took so much as a single step.

Day after day, the Prince kept the mermaid by his side. They walked together in the green forest or went riding among the hills. And never in all her life had the mermaid known such happiness. But although the Prince told her many times that he loved her, he loved her as he loved his small sisters. Not for one moment did he think of her as a wife.

One day the Prince told her that his counselors were saying that soon he must think of choosing a wife. "I have no wish to marry," he laughed. "I have my dear little orphan of the sea to keep me company and dance for me. Why should I marry?"

The little sea Princess could only nod and smile and she tried to keep smiling when the Prince went on. "It seems," he said, "that the king of a neighboring country has a very beautiful daughter who would make me a good wife. My Prime Minister says that it is my duty to visit this king and meet his daughter."

When the great ship that was to carry the Prince across the seas was fitted out, the Prince sent for the little mermaid. "I want you to come with me," he said. "I shall just take one look at this Princess and then return home. You will be my companion on the journey."

The little mermaid found it strange and wonderful to be sailing in a big ship across the ocean. Once, as she stood alone on the deck, she saw her five sisters come swimming through the water towards her. They looked up at her sadly and held out their white arms to her. But the little mermaid could not greet them with words. She could only smile and wave.

How anxiously she awaited the moment when the Prince would meet the new Princess face to face. Surely he would never be able to love her. Surely he would turn away and start making arrangements to return home. But, alas, when the mermaid saw the King's daughter waiting on the quayside to welcome the young Prince, she had to admit that this Princess was indeed beautiful. She was lovelier than any of the girls at the Prince's court.

By the end of the day, it was clear to everyone that the handsome young Prince was enchanted by the Princess. Not only was she very lovely but she was also kind and gracious and she was especially kind to the little mermaid.

After a few days, the Prince said to the mermaid, "I can see that you are growing to love the Princess. I know that already she loves you. When we marry, you shall live with us in the palace. Nothing will be changed."

For answer, the mermaid kissed the Prince's hand, hiding her eyes so that he would not see how her heart was breaking. She had failed to become his wife. The sea-witch had said that if the Prince married someone else, she would die. Soon she would be nothing more than white foam on the waves of the sea.

In great splendor, the Prince and the Princess were married and after the wedding they went aboard the ship so that the Prince could take his new wife home to his own palace. The little mermaid went with them, hiding her sadness.

That night the mermaid did not sleep. So great was her sorrow it seemed as if her heart was breaking, and she knew that with the first rays of the sun she would die. As she stood all alone on the deck of the great ship, she suddenly saw her sisters rise out of the sea. They were pale as death and their long beautiful hair no longer streamed out behind them in the wind.

"We have given our beautiful hair to the sea-witch," the eldest called out, above the noise of the wind, "so that we might bring you help. You need not die tonight, after all. The witch has given us her silver knife and you must thrust it into the Prince's heart before the sun rises. The blood that falls on your feet will change them back once more into a fish-tail. You will become a mermaid again and will return to us."

The silver knife fell at the mermaid's feet and as she picked it up her sisters dived under the waves. Like a shadow, the mermaid stole into the Prince's cabin where he slept with his lovely bride at his side. For a moment the little mermaid stood there, holding the knife over his heart. Then she turned away and fled from the cabin. Far, far out to sea, she threw the witch's knife and as it sank beneath the waves, she dived from the side of the ship and followed it.

But the grave little mermaid did not, after all, change to white foam on the waves. Her gentle heart had won for her a special place among the good spirits of the air.

"Where am I going?" she asked, as she found herself floating gently upwards. And the spirits told her, "You are one of us now because you loved and suffered so much."

In the morning, the Prince searched in vain for his dear little companion. "It is strange," he told his young wife. "Although she is nowhere to be found on the ship, I feel that she is still with me."

"I am, I am," whispered the little mermaid as she tenderly brushed his brow. But only the wind and the sea knew that she had spoken.

Ricky-of-the-Tuft

ONCE UPON a time there was a Queen who gave birth to a very ugly baby boy. Indeed, some of the ladies of the court vowed secretly that he was the ugliest baby in the whole world! The reason for his ugliness was a strange little tuft of hair that sprouted, like grass, out of the top of his head. Of course, no one dared to say how ugly he was in the presence of the Queen but she knew very well her baby was not nearly as pretty as others.

Now, although the baby was christened Richard, he soon became known as Ricky-of-the-Tuft which upset the Queen very much. At last she sent for the wisest fairy in the land.

"I cannot change the way your baby looks," said the wise fairy. "But I can give him a special gift. He will grow up to be very wise and very clever. What is more, if he falls in love with a stupid girl he will be able to give her some of his wisdom and cleverness."

Well, Ricky grew up and he was so wise and so clever that no one noticed his short legs, his long nose or the odd tuft of hair that sprouted out of his head.

One day an artist came to the palace and showed him a portrait of a most beautiful Princess. "She is indeed lovely," said Ricky. "I should very much like to meet her."

Then the artist told Ricky a strange story about the beautiful Princess who lived in a neighboring kingdom. "When she was born," said the artist, "she was said to be the most beautiful baby in the whole world. Her mother was so proud of her that she boasted to everyone about her beautiful new baby daughter. One day a wise fairy came to the palace to see the child and the proud Queen boasted to her too."

"A wise fairy came to see me when I was a baby," said Ricky, as he gazed at the picture.

"This fairy decided to punish the proud Queen," went on the artist. "She told her that the child would grow up to be very stupid. And the truth is, sire, that she is so stupid and so dull that no man wants to stay in her company for long. She can scarcely put four words together and so she is left very much alone."

Ricky gave the artist a great deal of money for the Princess's picture and in the weeks that followed spent much of his time standing in front of it, just gazing. At last he made up his mind to visit the lovely Princess and, if she were as beautiful as her picture, ask her to marry him.

As luck would have it, almost as soon as he had crossed the border into the neighboring kingdom, he came upon the Princess. She was walking in her favorite woods where she could be alone and far away from people who knew her to be stupid. And she looked so lonely and sad that Ricky's kind heart was immediately touched.

"You are three times more beautiful than your portrait," he told her, as he went up to her. "My name is Prince Ricky-of-the-Tuft and I have long wished to meet you."

The poor Princess was completely at a loss for words. She blushed and stammered and only managed to say, "I thank you." Then she stopped altogether.

"I know who you are," Ricky went on in his gentle voice. "And I want you to know that I love you."

"Alas," said the Princess, after a long silence. "I am the most stupid girl in the whole world. No man wants to stay with me for I have nothing to say . . ."

This was a very long speech for the Princess to make and she sank on to the grass and hid her face in her hands.

Ricky sat down beside her and presently the Princess found enough

courage to look at him carefully. His ugly face gave her some courage and she spoke again. "I have a sister," she told Ricky, "who is very plain, but she is so witty and clever that already she has had ten proposals of marriage."

"What would you give to be as clever and witty as your sister?" asked Ricky.

"Anything," answered the Princess. "All my beauty. . . ."

"If you could bring yourself to take me for your husband," said Ricky eagerly, "I could give you this gift of cleverness that you want so much."

The Princess plucked at the grass quite unable to make sense of what the odd little man was saying. But when Ricky repeated his words slowly and clearly, she looked up.

"You m-mean I c-could be clever?" she asked. "How? When?"

"You have only to promise to marry me," said Ricky, "and the gift is yours."

"I promise, I promise!" cried the Princess, her blue eyes shining. Then she added, "But not right away. . . ."

"Of course not," said Ricky. "I will give you a whole year to think about it. A year from now I will meet you in these same woods and ask you to keep your promise."

As Ricky stood up and pulled her to her feet, the Princess felt a powerful change come over her. Suddenly she found herself able to speak in a commanding and clever way. Words poured out of her mouth. She began to tell Ricky about her father and the laws he had passed to make his people happy.

Ricky-of-the-Tuft listened quietly, a smile on his ugly face. "Truly you are clever," he said. "You now have the gift I promised you. Go back to your father's palace and see how things will change."

Then, bowing low, he left her. The Princess ran all the way home. As soon as she was back in the palace she called the servants together and told them how they could perform their duties much faster if they followed the advice she was about to give them. They listened in amazement. Until that moment, they had looked upon the Princess as hopelessly stupid and treated her like a child.

That night, at dinner, the Princess talked with so much sense about the affairs of the kingdom that the King quite forgot to eat as he listened. As for the Queen, she was so delighted at her daughter's new-found cleverness that she almost fainted with joy.

Soon, the palace was crowded with handsome young men all begging the Princess to look upon them with favor. Day after day she astonished the people with her wisdom, and poets and writers recorded her sayings for posterity.

A whole year passed. The Princess knew that one day she must choose a husband from all the handsome young noblemen who came to the palace. But she could not make up her mind about any one of them. They all seemed equally handsome and equally pleasant. At last, to escape their attentions, she left the palace and went into the woods.

As she wandered among the trees, she was suddenly astonished to hear voices: "Frizzle the fry: Pit the pancake: Dip the dough."

"What nonsense is this?" thought the Princess, unable to make any sense out of the words that came to her ears. "And where can these voices be coming from?"

To her amazement, as she took a step forward the ground in front of her opened up and she found herself staring down into a vast, underground kitchen.

Little tiny men, no more than dwarf-height, were rushing hither and thither in tall hats and white aprons that reached to their feet.

Others, dressed all in green, were laying a long polished table with golden goblets and plates of gold and silver. Some of the little men were singing while they stirred the boiling pots and mixed dough, and some were making garlands of brightly colored flowers and leaves.

"Now, what can all this be about?" the Princess asked herself.

Presently, as she watched, several of the little men clambered up a long rope ladder and began gathering more leaves from the ground where she stood. They paid no attention to her and the Princess was forced to bend down and take one firmly by the arm. "Tell me," she said, "what are you all doing?"

"Don't you know?" said the little dwarf. "We are preparing a wedding feast for our friend and master, Ricky-of-the-Tuft. Our Prince is going to marry a beautiful Princess tomorrow and we want everything to be ready in time."

"Ricky – Ricky-of-the-Tuft!" the Princess repeated the name to herself, as she let go of the little man. Suddenly, she remembered her promise and all that had passed between Ricky and herself just a year ago.

If there had been time, the Princess would have run from the woods. But it was too late for as she turned she saw Prince Ricky himself coming towards her. He was so richly and finely dressed that it looked indeed as if he was going to a wedding!

"So you have remembered!" he exclaimed with a happy smile. "You have come to keep your promise."

"I have not!" cried the Princess, looking at the ugly little man with scorn. "That promise was given by a fool of a girl who never should have made it."

"A promise is a promise," said Ricky gently.

The Princess was silent for a moment for she knew that a promise should never be broken once it was given. "I was so stupid then," she said more quietly. "You will not try to hold me to a promise that I gave so long ago. Set me free of it, I beg you."

"I cannot and I will not," said Ricky. "I gave you the gift you longed for and in return you promised to be my wife."

The Princess was silent, remembering all the happiness Ricky's gift of cleverness had brought her. At last, she said, "It is true that I owe you a great deal and I could love you for that. But you are so ugly that I would not dare to take you home."

Ricky smiled. "If that is all!" he cried. "Then you, yourself, my beautiful Princess, can change my looks. I have learned since we met that the wise fairy gave you a special gift like the one she gave me.''

"What is it?" cried the Princess. "Tell me!"

"If you will but love me for myself," replied Ricky, "you can change this ugly creature you see before you into a handsome Prince."

"With all my heart I wish that this was so!" exclaimed the Princess. And no sooner had she spoken than Ricky-of-the-Tuft appeared before her as the most strikingly handsome man she had ever seen in her life.

"Now will you marry me?" asked Ricky, smiling.

"Yes, yes, indeed I will," whispered the Princess. "I know now I could not care for another man as I care for you."

So Ricky-of-the-Tuft and the beautiful Princess were married. They had two wedding feasts; one among the little people of the woods and the other at the Princess's palace where it was clear to everyone that the Princess was marrying the man she truly loved.

Did Ricky really grow into such a very handsome Prince? Some who know this story well have said that it was the Princess's true love for him that made him handsome, and that the wise fairy had very little to do with it . . . but we shall never really know.

The Flying Trunk

HERE WAS once a merchant, who was so rich that he had enough gold to build a castle. But he did not do so; instead he saved every gold piece he made and when he died he left his only son a vast fortune.

As soon as the son got the money he began to spend it. Every night he treated his friends to drinks and parties and just to show how little he cared about money, he would go down to the river and play at skipping stones using his gold pieces instead of pebbles. No wonder that, by the end of just one year, the merchant's huge fortune was gone and his son was left with four silver coins and no clothes to wear but an old dressing-gown and a pair of shabby slippers.

One day, as the young man sat alone in an empty house, having sold all his furniture to pay off his debts, the only friend he had left in the world came to see him. "I've brought you a present," he said. "It's an old trunk. You can pack your clothes in it and set about making your own fortune."

When his friend had left him, the young man thought, "That's all very well. But the only clothes I have to pack are this old dressing-gown and my slippers." And with a grim smile, he climbed into the trunk himself and sat down.

Now the trunk was really a magic trunk. If any one pressed the lock it could fly. Well, it wasn't long before the young man felt sleepy

and as he dozed off leaned against the lock. Hey presto! Away went the trunk. Up, up, up through the chimney and over the clouds and on and on, crossing two seas and flying over the tops of several high mountains.

In this way the merchant's son reached the Land of the Turks and having discovered that he could send the trunk down to earth by pressing the catch, he did so. The trunk landed in a forest and the young man climbed out.

Now, as everybody knows, the Turks at that time walked about in dressing-gowns and slippers so the merchant's son had no reason to feel odd as he left the forest and made his way towards the capital city.

Close to the city, he saw a magnificent castle whose only windows were very high up. "Tell me," he said, stopping the first Turkish lady he met on the road. "Who lives in that high castle?"

"Our Sultan keeps his daughter locked up in the tower," the woman told him. "It has been foretold by our star-gazers that the Princess will meet and marry a man who will bring her much unhappiness. The Sultan wishes to protect his daughter from such a man."

"Thank you," said the merchant's son. And he went back to the forest where he had buried his trunk, opened it and climbed in. Soon he was flying up towards the roof of the castle. The trunk made a perfect landing on the roof and the young man was able to climb through the Princess's window.

The Princess was lying asleep on the sofa and he saw at a glance that she was very beautiful. She was so beautiful that he could not stop himself from kissing her.

"Don't be frightened," he said, when the Princess opened her eyes and looked at him in terror. "I am a Turkish Angel. I have flown through the skies to be with you."

Now it seemed to the Princess that the young man must indeed be an angel – how else could he have entered her room? So she invited him to sit beside her on the sofa and allowed him to hold her slender hands.

The young man was a great story-teller. He talked about big cities where the men wore trousers instead of dressing-gowns, and he told stories of deep rivers and high snowy mountains. He told her about the storks who brought little children to lonely couples and beautiful Princesses who found their true loves among the angels.

Then he said, "Will you marry me?"

And the Princess said "Yes. But you must come here on Saturday. That is the day my Papa, the Sultan, and my Mamma, the Sultana, come to tea. They will be very proud that I am going to marry a Turkish Angel. Please make sure you can tell them a story for they like stories more than anything else."

"I shall bring a story instead of a marriage present," said he, getting ready to climb through the window. But before he went, the Princess gave him a splendid jeweled sword in a sheath embroidered with gold pieces.

With the gold pieces, the young man purchased a truly magnificent dressing-gown covered with stars and dragons, and also a new pair of slippers. Then he buried his flying trunk in the woods and spent the rest of the week wandering through the capital city, drinking thick, delicious Turkish coffee and eating a large number of tasty meals.

But although he enjoyed himself a lot, he did not stop thinking about the kind of story he would tell the Sultan and the Sultana on Saturday. "It must be a good one," he thought, "for much depends on it. If I can please the Sultan and Sultana they will surely allow me to marry their lovely daughter."

When Saturday afternoon came, the merchant's son climbed into his flying trunk, flew on to the roof and once again entered the Princess's room by the window. The Princess, her mother and father and several of the court ladies were already there, waiting for him. And, straightaway, he began his story.

"There was once," he said, "a bundle of Matches and the Matches were extremely proud of their ancestors. They said they came from a huge fir tree in the forest and that they were much better than anything else to be found in the old kitchen."

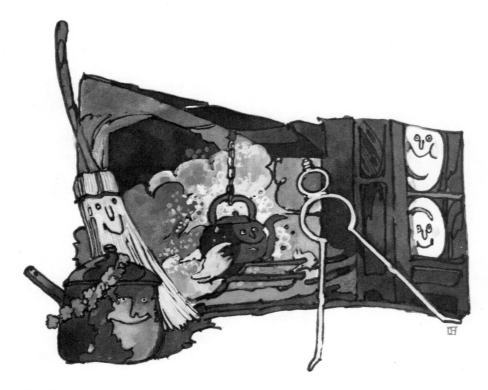

"I don't believe it," cried the Princess, clapping her hands. But the Sultan told her to be quiet.

"The Matches lay between a Tinder-Box and an old iron Pot," went on the story-teller. "When the Matches said what grand people they were, the iron Pot interrupted, saying that in many ways he was also very important. 'I was the first here in the house,' he declared, 'and my greatest pleasure is to sit in my place very clean and neat.'"

"I can understand the Pot's pleasure," cried one of the Court ladies, whose mother worked in the palace kitchens. "There is something very attractive about a pot that is well scoured and looks clean and shiny."

"The Matches," went on the merchant's son, paying no attention to the Court lady, "were so proud and thought so much of themselves that they would scarcely listen to the iron Pot as he tried to tell his story. But the Plates rattled with annoyance at the Matches and the Carpet Broom put a wreath of green parsley around the Pot just to teach the Matches a lesson. The Fire Tongs did a dance to draw attention to themselves and the Tea-Pot whistled a song. But all the Matches would say was, 'What common people we have to live among.' And then they refused to say anymore . . ."

"Pride comes before a fall," said the Sultana. "Do you know we have a Tea-Pot ourselves that sings whenever it is filled with boiling water."

"The Kettle had a better voice than the Tea-Pot," went on the

83

merchant's son. "And just to show the proud Matches what he thought of them, he sang a loud whistling song. It was so loud that the maid heard it and came running into the kitchen. She picked up the Matches and lit the fire with them. And, goodness me, you should have seen how they spluttered and burst into flames! 'Now, you can all see how important we are,' cried the last of the Matches. 'See how we shine!' But then he burned out and there was nothing left of him except a piece of useless charcoal."

The merchant's son stopped and looked at the Sultana. "What do you think of my story?" he asked.

"I enjoyed every word of it," she cried. "It reminded me of the days when I once served as a kitchen-maid before the Sultan fell in love with me . . ."

"Splendid story," declared the Sultan, and all the court ladies clapped their hands. "You shall marry our daughter."

So the wedding was arranged and on the evening before the great day, flags and colored lights were everywhere to be seen in the capital city. Cakes and sugar cookies were thrown among the people and everybody wore simply magnificent dressing-gowns. It was all so gay and splendid that the merchant's son began to wish that he, too, might do something special to give the people a treat.

"When I was a child," he thought, "I enjoyed a firework display best of all." And he went out and bought a great quantity of rockets and firecrackers and pinwheels and other splendid fireworks that gave off showers of golden rain. All these he put into his trunk and then flew up in it over the city.

"Crackle and Bang!" The people in the streets could hardly believe their eyes as they looked upwards and saw the dark sky ablaze with a thousand bright shooting stars. In their excitement children ran up and down shouting, "Hurrah! Hurrah! The Turkish Angel commands the stars to dance for us."

And their parents murmured among themselves, "To think our Princess is marrying an angel. We may look forward to wonderful things in the future."

The next day, in magnificent splendor, the merchant's son and the Princess were married and the wedding celebrations went on from early morning to late at night. At last, when the guests were falling asleep where they stood, the Princess went back to her high turret room, saying, "I will wait for you there," for her bridegroom had said that he wished to be alone for a short time.

The merchant's son hurried back to the forest, meaning to climb into his trunk and fly upwards to his bride. Alas, when he came to the spot where he had left it, he found a pile of ashes. A spark from his fireworks had landed on his wonderful trunk and it had burned away. Now, he could not fly to his lovely bride who was waiting for him. His days as a Turkish angel were over; and so too was his marriage!

Some say the Turkish Princess is still waiting for her Angel husband but others declare that, after ten years, the Sultana found her another suitable husband. All that is known for certain is that the merchant's son never returned to his own country but wandered through the lands of the East as a story-teller – although never again did he tell the story about the Matches. Most likely he wanted to forget the whole sad business.

Three Little Men of the Forest

ONCE UPON a time there lived an old shoemaker, whose wife had died. A year or so later, the shoemaker thought to himself, "I might as well marry again." The truth was that he had recently met a widow who also wished to marry.

Now the shoemaker had one lovely daughter called Catherine, and the widow had a plain daughter called Hilda. And the shoemaker hoped that the two girls would be friends. But the girls were as different as chalk is from cheese. Catherine was as gentle and kind as she was pretty, and Hilda – well, sad to say, Hilda was as mean and disagreeable as she was plain.

The shoemaker married the widow at the beginning of winter and as the weeks passed his new wife grew to hate her gentle stepdaughter. She hated her all the more when she saw her own daughter sitting beside her for then she could see with half-an-eye who was prettier.

As winter set in, the river was frozen as hard as stone and the valley was covered with snow. And it was then that the shoemaker's wife made a cloak out of paper for Catherine before sending her out into the bitter cold. "Fetch me a basketful of wild strawberries for nothing else will satisfy me," she told the girl. "And don't dare come back until you have found them."

"But the ground is frozen hard and the snow covers everything," poor Catherine cried, as she took the paper cloak and the basket. "Do you want me to freeze to death?"

For answer, her stepmother opened the door and pushed her out into the snow. "And see that your basket is full," she shouted, before slamming the door shut.

Catherine made for the forest where every blade of grass was hidden by the snow. There was not a strawberry to be seen and, at last, shivering with cold, she came to a cottage right in the middle of the woods. Here, three little Dwarfs lived and when they saw the girl at the door, they called out to her to come inside. Then they seated her by their fire, took off her paper cloak and asked if she had anything to eat in her basket.

"I have only a slice of bread," she answered. "That was all my step-mother would give me. But I will gladly share it with you." And she broke the bread into four tiny pieces and gave each of the Dwarfs a mouthful.

"What brings you into the forest on such a day?" one of the little men asked after they had eaten her bread.

"I must fill my basket with wild strawberries," Catherine said. "Thank you for taking me in. But now I must try once again to find some."

"We would like you to help us first by sweeping away the snow with this broom from our back door," said another of the Dwarfs, as Catherine rose to go. "Will you do that for us?"

"Of course I will," said Catherine, thinking that she would like to help such friendly little men. "It won't take long." And she took the broom and went outside.

When she had gone, the tallest of the Dwarfs whispered, "What can we give her? She has shared her bread with us and now she is sweeping away the snow."

"I'll grant that she becomes more beautiful every day," said the youngest and fattest of the Dwarfs.

"I'll grant that a piece of gold falls out of her mouth with every word she speaks," said the middle Dwarf.

"And I'll grant that a King's son shall come along and fall in love with her," said the tallest of the Dwarfs.

Then they fell silent as Catherine rushed into the room, her face alight with happiness. "Look!" she cried. "Look what I found as I swept away the snow. Lovely red strawberries!" And she held up her basket.

The three little men showed no surprise. Instead they wished her a pleasant journey home and as she ran down the path, they stood in the doorway and waved her goodbye.

Her stepmother, when she saw the strawberries, gave her no thanks but scolded her for taking so long. "I found a little cottage..." Catherine began and stopped for a shower of gold pieces had fallen out of her mouth and was lying at her feet.

"Goodness!" cried Hilda, who happened to come into the room.

"Whatever next! She's throwing gold about as if it was sugar! I suppose you just happened to find a bag of it in the forest?"

At this, Catherine, with some difficulty, told the whole story and by the end of it a fortune in gold pieces lay at her feet.

"Give me my cloak and let me go immediately into the forest," Hilda said to her mother, when Catherine had gone upstairs. "I'll find that cottage, and the Dwarfs will do the same for me as they have done for her."

So then her mother wrapped her daughter in a warm fur cloak, packed her basket with bread, meat and cake and allowed her to go into the woods.

Hilda found the cottage without any difficulty and knocked on the door. The three little men called out to her to enter. Then they seated her by the fire, took off her warm fur cloak and asked her if she had anything to eat in her basket.

"I have," said Hilda, who had, so far, not spoken a word of thanks.

"Will you share your food with us?" asked the tallest of the Dwarfs.

"Certainly not," snapped the girl. "I have scarcely enough to satisfy my own hunger." And with that she took the bread and meat out of her basket and began to eat it quickly. Then she ate the cake while the three little men silently watched her.

As soon as she had eaten the last crumb, they said to her. "Will you sweep away the snow from our back door? Here is a broom."

"Do your own sweeping," retorted Hilda rudely. "I'm not your servant!" And she tossed the broom into a corner. "Now," she continued, "I'll go outside and look for these wild strawberries that my stepsister found in your garden." And she clattered out of the cottage.

When she was gone, the Dwarfs said to each other, "What shall we give her? She is so rude and has such bad manners that we cannot wish her well." Then the tallest Dwarf said, "I'll grant that she grows more ugly every day." And the middle Dwarf said, "I'll grant that with every word she speaks a toad will drop out of her mouth." This, as you may know, is a favorite punishment of all dwarfs and fairies.

And the third and fattest of the little men said, "I'll grant that, one day, she gets a soaking in the river."

Hilda searched in vain for the strawberries and without bothering to thank the little men for allowing her to sit by their fire, she returned home in a very bad temper. Imagine her mother's fright when, with her very first angry words, three toads dropped from her mouth and began hopping over the kitchen floor!

Now, more than ever, Catherine was hated by her stepmother and the next day she gave her a net and an axe. "Take this net," she said, "and go to the pond. Cut a hole in the ice with the axe and drag the net through the water so that you may catch a fish. Don't dare to come home without any fish."

Poor Catherine's face was blue with cold and her fingers numb as

she ran to the pond, dragging the heavy net behind her. With the axe she cut a hole in the ice and then pulled the net through the water. But not a single fish did she catch.

Again and again she tried and was just about to give up when she heard the sound of horses' hooves on the road that ran beside the pond. She looked behind her and there was the King's carriage coming along at a rattling pace.

The young King stopped his carriage when he saw the beautiful young girl on the ice and beckoned her to come to him. "What are you doing?" he asked curiously.

"I must drag this net in the water and catch some fish," Catherine told him, a shower of gold pieces falling on the ice as she spoke.

Who knows if it was the gold or Catherine's gentle beauty that first attracted the handsome young King? At any rate he quickly invited her to ride with him back to his palace and by the end of the journey he was more than a little in love with her and she with him. And the very next day they were married.

A whole year passed in great happiness, particularly for the King, for Catherine not only grew more beautiful with every day but was forever dropping gold pieces which she gave him to spend on the poor people in his kingdom.

At the end of the year, a fine baby son blessed their marriage and the three little men of the forest came to the grand Christening Party, though they said not a word about their previous good wishes for the gentle Catherine.

As for the old shoemaker, in time he grew so weary of his nagging wife and ugly stepdaughter, who seemed to grow uglier every day, that, at last, he pushed them both into the river. "Don't ever come back," he shouted after them, as they scrambled up the far bank. "I'm sick and tired of you both *and* the toads. . ."

When the shoemaker found himself all alone, he made his way to the palace where he was joyfully received by his daughter. She gave him a splendid suite of rooms and a servant of his own and he stayed with her for the rest of his days and was very happy.